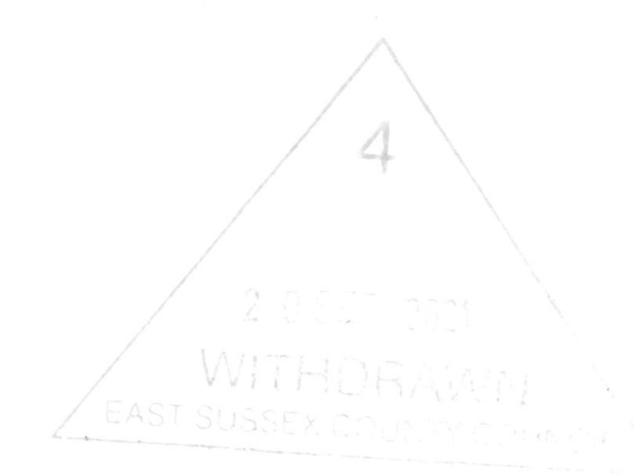

Dancing Maddy

First published in hardback in Great Britain by HarperCollins Publishers Ltd in 1999
First published in Picture Lions in 2000

1 3 5 7 9 10 8 6 4 2
ISBN: 0 00 6646700

Picture Lions is an imprint of the Children's Division, part of HarperCollins Publishers Ltd.

A CIP catalogue record for this title is available from the British Library.

The HarperCollins website address is: www.**fire**and**water**.com

Printed in Singapore by Imago

Dancing Maddy

Clare Jarrett

PictureLions

An Imprint of HarperCollins*Publishers*

Mrs Lamb was planning the school show.

Lee and Jack were ponies. Rosie and Emily were fairies and the others were clowns.

Maddy plucked up courage to ask Mrs Lamb.

"Please can I do my princess dance?"

"What a lovely idea," said Mrs Lamb. "We need a princess in the show."

So Maddy danced her princess dance,
but it went wrong.

She lost her balance and fell over.
"Don't laugh, Jack," said Mrs Lamb.

Maddy was still
miserable when
Mummy came
to take her home.
"Cheer up, darling,
it's not the end of
the world."

Maddy went into the garden.
She looked up and saw a speck
in the sky.

She watched as a parachute
floated slowly down.

"Hello there!" called the dog.
"I'm Pomeroy, you must be Maddy."

Maddy smiled. "Hello," she said.

She helped him take off the parachute. She loved the brilliant colours and the silky feel of the material.

"It must be lunchtime," said Pomeroy. "I'm *very* hungry."

"Yes," said Maddy, "come and have lunch with me."

"Now," said Pomeroy, helping himself to food. "Why were you looking so sad?"

Maddy told him all about it.

"I never want to dance again," she said.

"That's serious," said Pomeroy. "Perhaps I can help."

He jumped up and danced across the room. Maddy was astonished.

"You see, I *love* dancing," he said. "Sometimes it goes wrong, but you must keep trying. Come on!"

Maddy started to dance slowly.

"Good," said Pomeroy, encouragingly.

Soon she was twirling and pirouetting. Pomeroy took her hand and they danced together.

Through the house they danced –
upstairs, downstairs…

and round the garden, until they landed in a heap, completely out of breath and laughing.

The clock struck three.

"Oh no," said Maddy, "the show!"

"I can't do my dance, I haven't got a dress."
"Don't worry," said Pomeroy. "I've got an idea."

He sat down and drew a picture of a beautiful dress.

Then he fetched the parachute.

“This will be perfect,” said Pomeroy.

They started to cut and sew. They used up the whole parachute, apart from a small piece which they made into a waistcoat for Pomeroy. Maddy stuck on sequins that flashed and glittered in the light.

Maddy put on the dress, Pomeroy tied the sash into an enormous bow.

“It’s beautiful,” she exclaimed.

“I think we are ready,” Pomeroy said, admiring himself.

“Maddy,” called Mummy, “you’d better get your skates on if you’re going to the show.”

Maddy and Pomeroy put on their roller skates and skated to school arm in arm.

"Ah, there you are Maddy," said Mrs Lamb. "What a perfect dress for your dance. I'm sure it will go really well this time. Now, are you ready?"

Maddy took a deep breath.

"Yes," she said.

Maddy felt nervous. She could see her family in the second row.

"Just enjoy dancing," said Pomeroy quietly.

Maddy began to dance. At last she was the Dancing Princess.

The audience clapped and cheered.
"I knew you could do it," whispered Pomeroy. He pulled a rose from his buttonhole and gave it to her.

"Thank you, Pomeroy," said Maddy, hugging him.

"I've got to go now," he said. "Remember, I will always be here if you need me."

"Goodbye, Pomeroy," whispered Maddy.

He turned and smiled as he vanished into the crowd.